SALINA PUBLIC LIBRARY

MW00700053

Little Badger's Just-About Birthday

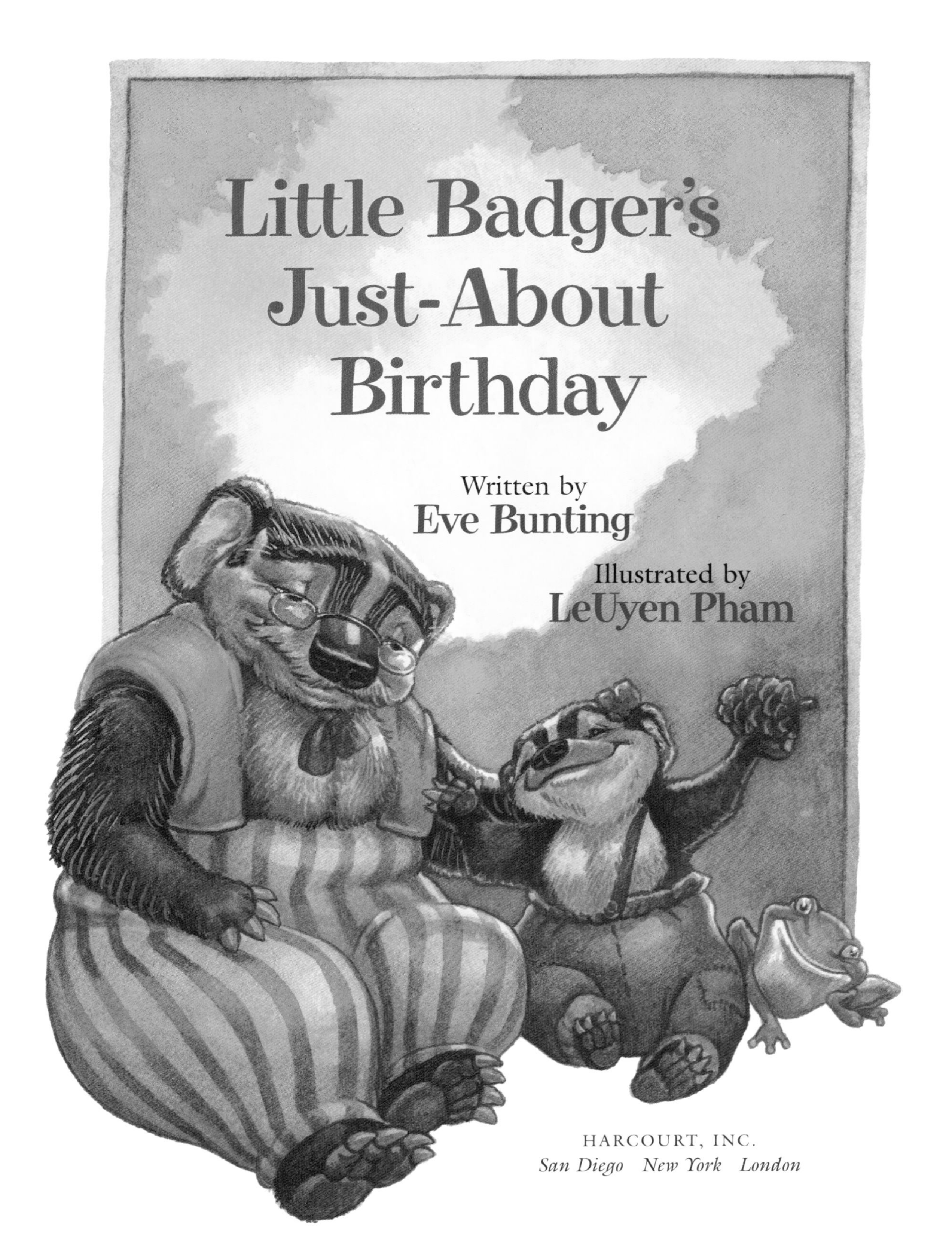

Written by
Eve Bunting

Illustrated by
LeUyen Pham

HARCOURT, INC.
San Diego New York London

Requests for permission to make copies of any part of the work should be mailed to the following address: Permissions Department, Harcourt, Inc., 6277 Sea Harbor Drive, Orlando, Florida 32887-6777.

www.harcourt.com

Library of Congress Cataloging-in-Publication Data
Bunting, Eve, 1928–
Little Badger's just-about birthday/
written by Eve Bunting;
illustrated by LeUyen Pham.
p. cm.
Summary: At his own "just-about" birthday party, Little Badger discovers that his friends have birthdays at just about the same time as his and thoughtfully figures out how everyone can celebrate their "just-about" birthdays and go home with a special present.
[1. Birthdays—Fiction. 2. Parties—Fiction.
3. Badgers—Fiction. 4. Animals—Fiction.]
I. Pham, LeUyen, ill. II. Title.
PZ7.B91527Lj 2002
[E]—dc21 2001001153
ISBN 0-15-202609-6

H G F E D C B A

Printed in Singapore

The illustrations in this book were done in gouache on Arches 200-pound rough press watercolor paper.
The display type was set in Elroy.
The text type was set in Galliard.
Color separations by Bright Arts Ltd., Hong Kong
Printed and bound by Tien Wah Press, Singapore
This book was printed on totally chlorine-free Nymolla Matte Art paper.
Production supervision by Sandra Grebenar and Ginger Boyer
Designed by Lori McThomas Buley and Suzanne Fridley

For James
Ryan Bunting,
on his just-about
birthday
-e.b.
For Brian Faiola
with all my
love
-L.P.

It was the time between dark and first light. Old Badger shook Little Badger's shoulder.

"Wake up, my Little Badger," he said. "Today is your just-about birthday."

Little Badger yawned. "What is *that*?"

"It was just about this time of the year, a while back, that you were born."

"Really?" Little Badger sat up. "You remember?"

"I remember." Old Badger took something from behind his back. It was a big, bristly, dry-as-dirt pine cone. "This is for you, Little Badger. It's your just-about birthday gift."

Little Badger held it up to the light. "It's the biggest, bristliest, dry-as-dirt pine cone ever! We can play catch, and kick-the-cone." He tossed it to Old Badger and Old Badger tossed it back.

"Good catch, Little Badger," he said. "Now it's time to get ready for your just-about birthday party."

Little Badger did a small dance. "Yippee!" he said.

Little Badger made three invitations. They said:

Please come to
my just-about
birthday party
today, in the
clearing.
Signed,
little Badger

He delivered them himself.
“I will certainly come,” said Woodchuck.
“And I will certainly come,” Crow cawed.
“Wouldn’t miss it,” Chipmunk chittered.

Please
my

Old Badger and Little Badger swept the clearing. They laid out honey clumps and sun-dried nuts and crispy crimped worms on their log table.

"Crow loves crispy crimped worms," Little Badger said happily. He picked a bluebell that was blue as the summer sky and that smelled of the damp, dark woods. He tucked it behind his ear so everyone would know he was the just-about birthday badger.

Chipmunk was the first to arrive. “Happy just-about birthday!” he told Little Badger. “I’ve brought you a present. I rolled it in the grass to get the slime off.” He laid the biggest, fattest chafer grub on the table.

“Oh, yum!” Little Badger licked his lips.

Woodchuck padded in, carrying a bright green acorn. "If you plant it, it will be a tree someday," he said.

Little Badger clapped his paws. "My very own tree!" He placed the bright green acorn on the log table. "Don't grow to be a tree until after the party," he told it.

Crow swooped down with a pale, pale moonstone.

"It looks like a piece of river ice," Little Badger said.

"I found it once, hidden in the earth," Crow said. "I've kept it safe in my nest for a long, long time."

Little Badger looked around at his friends. "This is the most perfect just-about birthday. Thank you all."

"You know," Crow cawed. "I think this is my just-about birthday, too. I broke through the shell of my egg on a day like today, many years ago."

Little Badger gasped. "You did?"

"And I think it's my just-about birthday, too," Woodchuck said. "My mother once told me I first opened my eyes on a soft, summer-coming day like this one."

"Really?" Chipmunk said. "I was born on a sunshiny day, too, when the frosts were gone and the buds were ripening."

Little Badger hopped a little hop. “It’s everybody’s just-about birthday! So the party is for everyone.”

They ate and ate.

They played hide-and-seek, and follow-the-leader, and king-of-the-hill, and kick-the-cone.

When they were too tired to play anymore, Little Badger said, "I've decided. Each of you must take home one of my presents."

"Oh no," Woodchuck said.

"Oh no," Crow cawed.

"Couldn't possibly," Chipmunk chittered.

But Little Badger told them that was what he wanted. "Besides, I still have my big, bristly, dry-as-dirt pine cone. It's from Old Badger and I'd like to keep it," he said.

So they each took one present home—but not the one they'd brought.

Little Badger and Old Badger tidied the clearing. They waddled to the pond and washed the honey from their paws. They sucked their claws to get the last crumbs of crispy crimped worms.

"Old Badger," Little Badger said, "when is *your* just-about birthday?"

Old Badger rubbed his chin. "Why, it must be just about now. All the badgers of the world since time began were born just about this time of year."

"Oh my! And you didn't get a present today!" Little Badger took the bluebell from behind his ear. It was limp and droopy, but it still held the colors of the summer sky. When he sniffed it, he could still smell the damp, dark woods.

He reached high, tucked it behind Old Badger's ear, and hugged him tight. "Happy just-about birthday."

"Thank you, my Little Badger."

Old Badger took Little Badger's paw and led him toward their burrow.

"Oh no!" Little Badger said. "It *can't* be time for bed."

Old Badger smiled. "It can," he said. "Just about."